Cornelius Vandermouse
The Pride of Newport

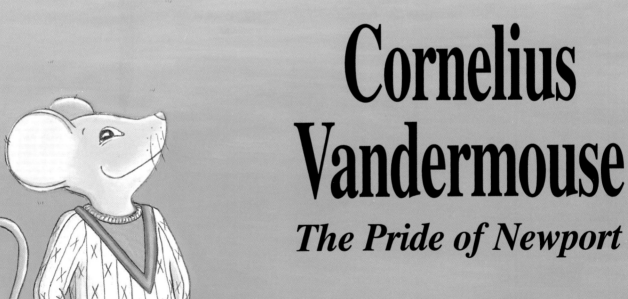

Written by
Peter W. Barnes *and*
Cheryl Shaw Barnes

Illustrated by
Susan Arciero

Edited by
Shirley F. Riess

Other books by Peter and Cheryl Barnes from VSP Books:

Woodrow, the White House Mouse, about the presidency and the nation's most famous
       mansion.
House Mouse, Senate Mouse, about Congress and the legislative process.
Marshall, the Courthouse Mouse, about the Supreme Court and the judicial process.
A "Mice" Way to Learn About Government teachers' curriculum guide, for the three books
       above.
Capital Cooking with Woodrow and Friends, a cookbook for kids that mixes fun recipes with fun
       facts about American history and government.
Woodrow For President, about how Woodrow the White House Mouse got to the White House.
A "Mice" Way to Learn about Voting, Campaigns and Elections teachers' curriculum guide, for
       Woodrow for President
Alexander, the Old Town Mouse, about historic Old Town, Alexandria, Va., across the Potomac
       River from Washington, D.C.
Nat, Nat, the Nantucket Cat (with Susan Arciero), about beautiful Nantucket Island, Mass.
Martha's Vineyard (with Susan Arciero), about wonderful Martha's Vineyard, Mass.

Also from VSP Books

Mosby, the Kennedy Center Cat, by Beppie Noyes, based on the true story of a wild stage cat that
       lived in the Kennedy Center in Washington D.C. (Autographed copies not available.)
M is for Maryland, by Carla Golembe, an alphabet book about Maryland. (Autographed copies
       not available.)

Order these books through your local bookstore by title,
or order **autographed copies** of the Barnes' books by calling **1-800-441-1949**,
or from our website at **www.VSPBooks.com**.

For a brochure and ordering information, write to:

VSP Books
P.O. Box 17011
Alexandria, VA 22302

To get on our mailing list, send your name and address to the address above.

ISBN 0-9637688-5-9

Library of Congress Catalog Card Number: 97-060529

10 9 8 7 6 5 4 3

Printed in the United States of America

Acknowledgments

We wish to thank many people for their time and help in the
development of this book, especially Countess Anthony
Szapary, whose input was invaluable, and Paul F. Miller,
curator of the Preservation Society, who reviewed every
illustration for its architectural and historic accuracy.

The Breakers

One beautiful day, the sun high above
   The grandest of Newport's grand houses
There walked on the lawn young Cornelius,
   Of Newport's renowned Vandermouses.

So handsome and modest, so bright and behaved,
   The pride of his Mother and Dad,
Cornelius was also athletic and brave—
   He was really a prince of a lad!

Like past Vandermouses, his skill was unmatched
    When he sailed a big ship called a "yacht."
Each summer, he raced every yacht race in town,
    And he won them more often than not!

A yacht is quite long, with a very tall sail—
    It hangs from a very tall mast.
A very good sailor commanding the wheel
    Can make it go far, very fast!

Cornelius was nervous and jumpy that day,
    Excited about something fun—
In only a day was the season's big race—
    A race that he never had won!

The name of the race was the Commodore's Cup.
    And here's why the fluster and bother—
The Commodore who had created the race
    Was Cornelius' own dear grandfather!

"I sail every year in my grandfather's race,"
    Cornelius said, "and I'm stuck.
I've practiced so much, what I really need now
    Is something to bring me good luck!"

Grandfather

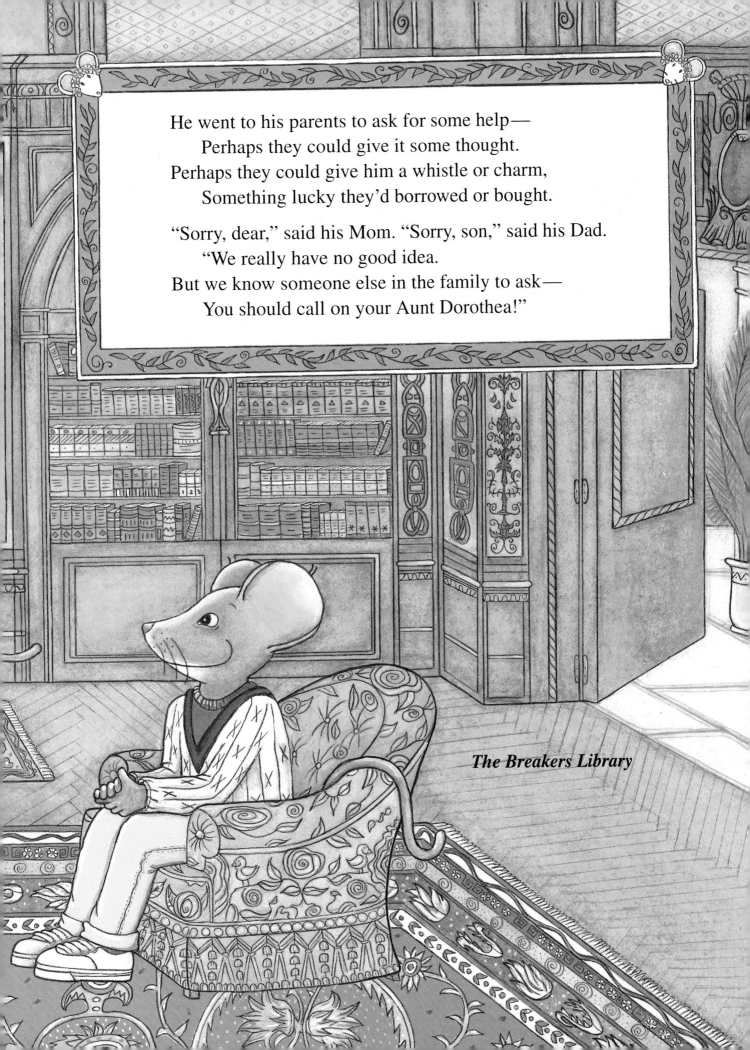

He went to his parents to ask for some help—
　　Perhaps they could give it some thought.
Perhaps they could give him a whistle or charm,
　　Something lucky they'd borrowed or bought.

"Sorry, dear," said his Mom. "Sorry, son," said his Dad.
　　"We really have no good idea.
But we know someone else in the family to ask—
　　You should call on your Aunt Dorothea!"

The Breakers Library

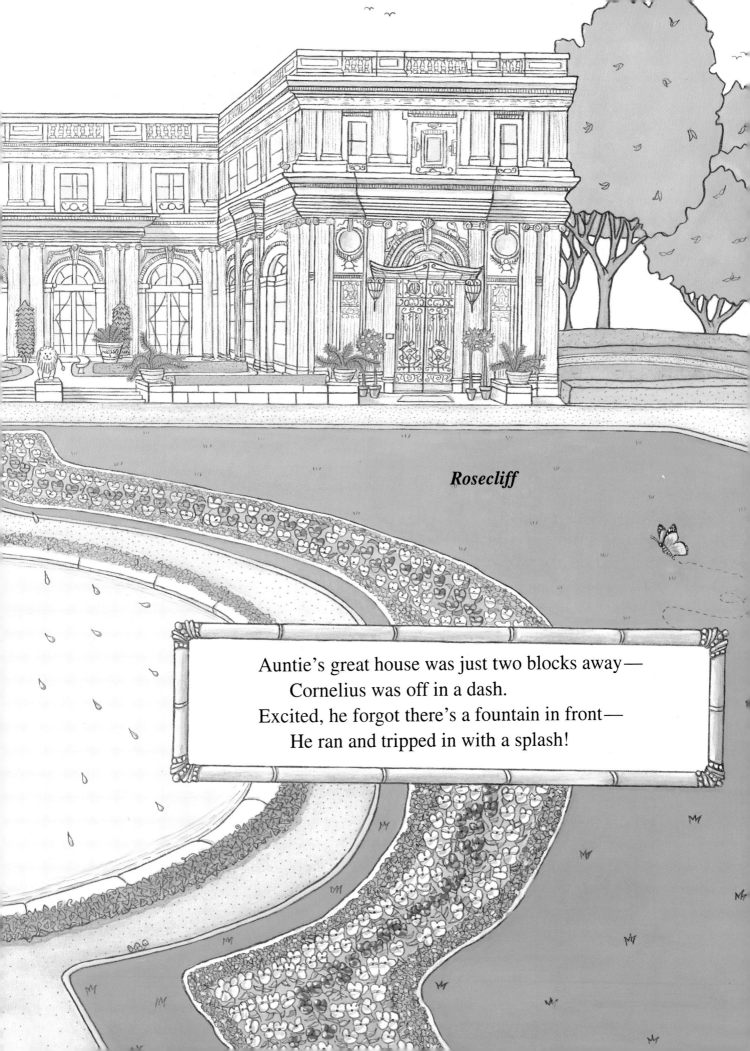

Rosecliff

Auntie's great house was just two blocks away—
Cornelius was off in a dash.
Excited, he forgot there's a fountain in front—
He ran and tripped in with a splash!

His aunt pulled him out, took him into the house,
    Dried him off, and then gave him a kiss.
"My goodness, dear nephew!" she said with a laugh,
    "What's the trouble? Is something amiss?"

Cornelius explained that he needed a charm,
    A trinket, or thingamajig—
Something *lucky* to win him the *Commodore's Cup*!
    (But not quite as shiny or big…)

His aunt thought a moment, and then thought some more,
    Then said, "Dear, I haven't a clue.
But I know that your Uncle, who lives right next door,
    Can come up with the thing that will do!"

Marble House

His Uncle Sebastian, a regular chap,
    Made his millions importing Swiss cheese.
He greeted Cornelius in front of his house,
    With, "Hello! Come in, nephew, please!"

The Gold Ballroom

Cornelius recounted his search for a charm—
Something lucky—a bauble or ring.
Sebastian, all ears, said, "Dear boy, follow me!
I believe I could have just the thing!"

"I've kept it for years," Sebastian declared.
    "Right here, in its own special place—
It's your grandfather's very own Commodore's cap—
    When he wore it, he won every race!"

Cornelius was thrilled! "My grandfather's cap!
    Why, thank you, Sebastian!" he said.

And as the race started that very next day,
It sat on Cornelius' head.

His crew heard the signal—a small cannon blast—
He was off, as the wind whipped the sail!
Cornelius held fast to the wheel of the boat,
With his hands and his very strong tail!

An hour had passed—two yachts were ahead
　　Of Captain Cornelius and crew.
The Commodore's grandson asked himself then,
　　"Now what would my grandfather do?"

And just at that moment, a strong gust of wind
　　Caught the rim of his grandfather's hat.
Cornelius turned fast, caught the wind in his sail,
　　And was leading in 10 seconds flat!

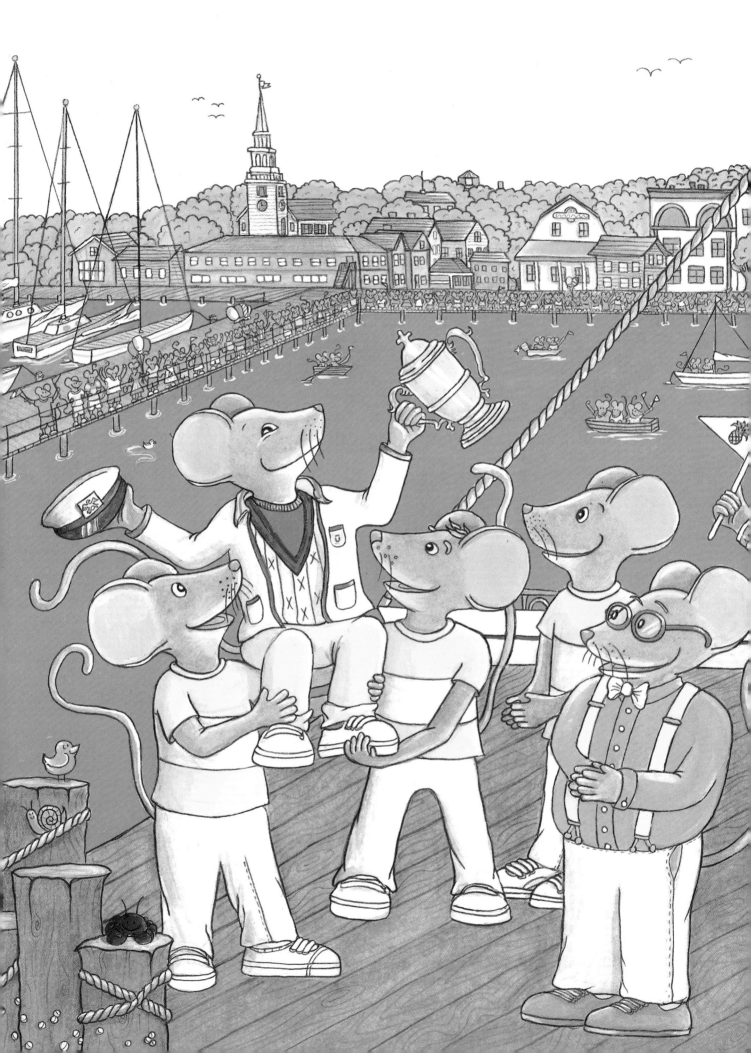

Just two minutes later, he crossed the line first,
    And two minutes more after that,
Cornelius was holding the Commodore's Cup
    And waving the Commodore's hat!

"Hooray!" the crowd shouted. "Three cheers!" someone said.
    Then everyone started to clap.
Cornelius just smiled and thought, "Dear Grandfather,
    It was all thanks to you and your cap."

Historical Notes for Parents and Teachers

Newport: The name conjures visions of grand mansions and superb sailing. And the story of Cornelius Vandermouse revolves around these two great historic traditions of this famous Rhode Island port city. Of course, Newport's history involves more than just water sports and architecture. The city was founded in 1639 by a group of colonists from Massachusetts, who settled on the south end of Aquidneck Island ("Isle of Peace" to the Native Americans who lived there), on the excellent natural harbor on Narragansett Bay. Early Newport flourished commercially and culturally. It was a major exporting and shipbuilding center and rivaled Boston, New York and Philadelphia as a colonial trading city. Because of its climate, location and culture, it quickly became a popular destination for vacationers and travelers.

But the Revolutionary War and the decline in maritime trade left Newport isolated and in hard times. It wasn't until after the Civil War that tourists and summer residents returned. In the late 1800s, Newport experienced its "Gilded Age," as the summer home of the rich and powerful. With them came great mansions—"cottages," to the captains of industry who built them—and recreation, especially sailing. The first sailing races, or "regattas," began in 1844. The residents raced yachts, though the term "yacht" is broadly defined as any boat used for recreational, rather than commercial, purposes. The yachts raced in Newport were not just vessels—they were sleek, fast sailboats. Newport also has been home to the triennial America's Cup race. Today, sailing remains one of the city's leading recreational activities.

In this book, the main character is named after Cornelius Vanderbilt, who created a steamship and railroad empire in the mid-1800s to become America's richest man. He was known as "The Commodore." His grandsons, Cornelius II and William, built two of the great stone "cottages" in Newport—respectively, The Breakers and Marble House.

The story of Cornelius Vandermouse opens outside **The Breakers**, where Cornelius lives with his parents. Designed by Newport's most renowned architect, Richard Morris Hunt, The Breakers was built in two years and opened in 1895. It is modeled after Renaissance palaces in Italy. The four-story limestone structure contains 70 rooms and covers nearly an acre of the 12-acre estate, located on Ochre Point. Inside the house, Cornelius worries about the next day's sailboat race under the gaze of his grandfather's portrait, which hangs in the staircase in the mansion's Great Hall. Next, Cornelius meets his parents in the library. The most striking feature of the room is the great stone fireplace, which originally came from a 16th-century French chateau.

After talking to his parents, Cornelius runs off to visit his aunt at **Rosecliff**, located along Newport's famous Bellevue Avenue, the address of many other great houses. The mansion is modeled after the 17th-century French garden retreat built at Versailles for Louis XIV. Construction began in 1898 and was completed in 1902. It has 30 rooms, but the most spectacular is the ballroom, which measures 40 feet wide and 80 feet long (Cornelius dries off there after his fall in the fountain).

Cornelius next visits his uncle at **Marble House**, built with a rich variety of rare marbles between 1888 and 1892, at an estimated cost of $11 million. It is modeled after the Petit Trianon Pavillion at Versailles. Its steel and bronze entrance grille is 20 feet long and 16 feet high and weighs 10 tons. Its most spectacular room is the famous Gold Ballroom, perhaps the greatest symbol of America's Gilded Age. Cornelius and his uncle walk through the Gold Ballroom to get to the mansion's beautiful library. On the grounds of the estate, overlooking the Cliff Walk, sits the **Chinese Teahouse**, built in 1913. In the story, the teahouse can be seen in the background during the yacht race. Other "cottages" in the background during the race are **Ochre Court** (built 1892) and **Vinland** (built 1883), now both academic buildings of Salve Regina University, and **Beechwood** (built 1853).

Most of the mansions featured in this book are owned and operated by The Preservation Society of Newport County, a private, not-for-profit educational organization founded in 1945. It controls eight properties, including The Breakers, Marble House and Rosecliff. For more information about the cottages and Newport, write the Society at 424 Bellevue Avenue, Newport, RI 02840, or call the Society at 401-847-1000.